Sports Superstars

LeBron James

Basketball Star

Mary Ann Hoffman

Published in 2007 by The Rosen Publishing Group, Inc.
29 East 21st Street, New York, NY 10010

Copyright © 2007 by The Rosen Publishing Group, Inc.

Book Design: Daniel Hosek

Photo Credits: Cover © Jonathan Daniel/Getty Images; pp. 5, 11 © Hector Mata/MATA/AFP/ Getty Images; p. 7 © Tom Pidgeon/Getty Images; pp. 9, 21 © Andy Lyons/Getty Images; p. 13 © Ezra Shaw/Getty Images; p. 15 © James Nielsen/AFP/Getty Images; p. 17 © Lisa Blumenfeld/ Getty Images; p. 19 © Otto Greule Jr./Getty Images.

Library of Congress Cataloging-in-Publication Data

Hoffman, Mary Ann, 1947-
  LeBron James : basketball star / Mary Ann Hoffman.
      p. cm. — (Sports superstars)
  Includes index.
  ISBN-13: 978-1-4042-3535-3
  ISBN-10: 1-4042-3535-3
  1. James, LeBron—Juvenile literature. 2. Basketball players—United States—Biography—Juvenile literature. I. Title. II. Series.
  GV884.J36H63 2007
  796.323092—dc22
  (B)
                                    2006014596

Manufactured in the United States of America

Contents

1   NBA Star   4

2   High School Star   6

3   Top Pick   8

4   The Olympics   12

5   All-Star   14

6   Strong and Quick   16

  Glossary   22

  Books and Web Sites   23

  Index   24

LeBron James is an NBA star!
He is only 22 years old!

LeBron was a high school star too. A national newspaper named him High School Basketball Player of the Year in 2002 and 2003!

LeBron was the first player picked in the 2003 NBA draft. He was picked by the Cleveland Cavaliers.

LeBron was named NBA Rookie of the Year in 2004. He was only 19!

LeBron was the youngest member of the 2004 USA Olympic team. Team USA took third place.

13

LeBron was the MVP in the 2006 NBA All-Star Game. That means he was the best player.

LeBron is a strong basketball player. He can jump very high.

17

LeBron is a quick basketball player. He can run very fast.

LeBron is very powerful. In 2004 and 2005, he played more minutes than any other player in the NBA!

Glossary

All-Star (AHL–STAHR) One of the best players in a sport.

draft (DRAFT) The way pro sports teams pick new players.

NBA (EN-BEE-AY) The National Basketball Association.

Olympic team (uh-LIHM-pihk TEEM) A team that plays other teams from around the world in the Olympics. The Olympics take place every 4 years.

powerful (POW-uhr-fuhl) Having great power and strength.

rookie (RU-kee) Someone who is in their first year in a sport.

Books and Web Sites

BOOKS:

Hareas, John. *LeBron James*. New York: Scholastic, 2005.

Mattern, Joanne. *LeBron James: Young Basketball Star.* Hockessin, DE: Mitchell Lane Publishing, 2004.

WEB SITES:

Due to the changing nature of Internet links, PowerKids Press has developed an online list of Web sites related to the subject of this book. This site is updated regularly. Please use this link to access the list:

http://www.powerkidslinks.com/spsuper/james/

Index

A

All-Star Game, 14

C

Cleveland Cavaliers, 8

D

draft, 8

H

High School Basketball
   Player of the Year, 6

M

MVP, 14

N

NBA, 4, 8, 10, 14, 20

O

Olympic team, 12

P

powerful, 20

Q

quick, 18

R

Rookie of the Year, 10

S

strong, 16